This Book Belongs to...

_____

© Illus. Dr. Seuss 1957

MARC BROWN

GLASSES FOR D.W.

BEGINNER BOOKS
A division of Random House, Inc.

Text and illustrations copyright © 1996 by Marc Brown.
All rights reserved under International and Pan-American Copyright Conventions.
Published in the United States by Random House, Inc., New York, and
simultaneously in Canada by Random House of Canada Limited, Toronto. Originally
published by Random House, Inc., in 1996 as a Step into Reading® Book.

Library of Congress Cataloging-in-Publication Data
Brown, Marc Tolon.   Glasses for D.W. / written and illustrated by Marc Brown.
p.   cm.   SUMMARY: Arthur's little sister wants to wear glasses like her brother and
tries to prove she needs them.   ISBN 0-679-86740-6 (pbk.). — ISBN 0-679-96740-0
(lib. bdg.).
[1. Eyeglasses—Fiction.   2.Anteaters—Fiction.   3. Brothers and sisters—Fiction.]
I. Title.   PZ7.B81618G1   1996   [E]—dc20 95-25763

Printed in the United States of America 10 9 8 7 6 5 4 3 2 1

Arthur wore glasses.
"I wish I wore glasses too,"
said his little sister, D.W.
"They look cool."

"But I really need them
to see," said Arthur.
"Before I wore glasses,
things looked funny."

"A hat looked like...
a bat.

Some string looked like...
a ring.

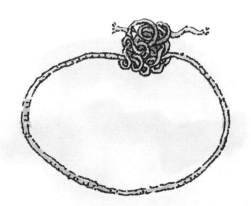

Some trash looked like…
some cash.

A log looked like…
a dog," said Arthur.

"Things look funny
to me too," said D.W.

"Remember last summer
when I saw the shark
at the beach...

"...and no one else did?
The nice lifeguard said,
'Maybe you need glasses,
little girl,'" said D.W.

"And Mom always tells me
I can't see what a mess
my room is," said D.W.
"Maybe glasses would help."

"You need more than glasses
to clean up that mess,"
said Arthur.

"I never can find my toothbrush,"
said D.W.
"And Daddy says
it's because I'm blind as a bat.
See, that means I need glasses."

"No," said Arthur.
"It just means you don't like
to brush your teeth."

"I REALLY do need glasses!"
said D.W.
She took two steps
and bumped into the lamp.

She took three more steps
and bumped into Arthur.
"I can't even see YOU, Arthur!"
cried D.W.

"Try opening your eyes,"
said Arthur.

Just then Arthur's friend Buster

came over.

"D.W. is acting silly,"

Arthur said to Buster.

D.W. took two steps
and bumped into Buster.
"Buster? Is that you?"
she said.
"Guess what? I can't see!"

"So I'm getting glasses!"
said D.W.

"Orange glasses that sparkle...
love glasses...

sunglasses...

rainglasses...

zillions of glasses!"

Buster gave D.W. a funny look.
"She's nuts, Arthur,"
said Buster. "Come on,
let's play soccer."

D.W. opened her eyes.
"I want to play too,"
she said.

"You can't play soccer
if you can't see,"
said Arthur.
D.W. grabbed the soccer ball.
She bounced it up and down.

"Who says I can't see?" said D.W.

"Hooray!" yelled Arthur.

"She can see again.

   It's the miracle soccer cure!"

"But I still want glasses,"
said D.W.

I CAN READ IT ALL BY MYSELF

Beginner Books